DANCE TRAP

by Diana G. Gallagher

illustrated by Brann Garvey

Librarian Reviewer
Laurie K. Holland
Media Specialist (National Board Certified), Edina, MN
MA in Elementary Education, Minnesota State University, Mankato

Reading Consultant
Elizabeth Stedem
Educator/Consultant, Colorado Springs, CO
MA in Elementary Education, University of Denver, CO

STONE ARCH BOOKS
MINNEAPOLIS SAN DIEGO

Claudia Cristina Cortez is published by Stone Arch Books
151 Good Counsel Drive, P.O. Box 669
Mankato, Minnesota 56002
www.stonearchbooks.com

Copyright © 2008 by Stone Arch Books

Library of Congress Cataloging-in-Publication Data
Gallagher, Diana G.
    Dance Trap: The Complicated Life of Claudia Cristina Cortez / by Diana
G. Gallagher; illustrated by Brann Garvey.
      p. cm. — (Claudia Cristina Cortez)
      Summary: As a member of the seventh-grade dance committee, Claudia
tries to find a way to convince the boys to attend the dance, which she knows
they will not do if Anna, another committee member, gets her way and makes
the event semi-formal.
      ISBN-13: 978-1-59889-841-5 (library binding)
      ISBN-10: 1-59889-841-8 (library binding)
      ISBN-13: 978-1-59889-879-8 (paperback)
      ISBN-10: 1-59889-879-5 (paperback)
      [1. Dance—Fiction. 2. Middle schools—Fiction. 3. Schools—Fiction.
4. Interpersonal relations—Fiction. 5. Cooperativeness—Fiction.] I. Garvey,
Brann, ill. II. Title.
PZ7.G13543Dan 2008
[Fic]—dc22   2007005953

Art Director: Heather Kindseth
Graphic Designer: Kay Fraser

Photo Credits
Delaney Photography, cover

1 2 3 4 5 6 11 10 09 08 07 06

Printed in the United States of America

Table of Contents

Cast of

ME

CLAUDIA

That's me. I'm thirteen, and I'm in the seventh grade at Pine Tree Middle School. I live with my mom, my dad, and my brother, Jimmy. I have one cat, Ping-Ping. I like music, baseball, and hanging out with my friends.

MONICA

MONICA is my very best friend. We met when we were really little, and we've been best friends ever since. I don't know what I'd do without her! Monica loves horses. In fact, when she grows up, she wants to be an Olympic rider!

BECCA

BECCA is one of my closest friends. She lives next door to Monica. Becca is really, really smart. She gets good grades. She's also really good at art.

ADAM and I met when we were in third grade. Now that we're teenagers, we don't spend as much time together as we did when we were kids, but he's always there for me when I need him. (Plus, he's the only person who wants to talk about baseball with me!)

ADAM

Characters

TOMMY's our class clown. Sometimes he's really funny, but sometimes he is just annoying. Becca has a crush on him . . . but I'd never tell.

I think **PETER** is probably the smartest person I've ever met. Seriously. He's even smarter than our teachers! He's also one of my friends. Which is lucky, because sometimes he helps me with homework.

Every school has a bully, and **JENNY** is ours. She's the tallest person in our class, and the meanest, too. She always threatens to stomp people. No one's ever seen her stomp anyone, but that doesn't mean it hasn't happened!

ANNA is the most popular girl at our school. Everyone wants to be friends with her. I think that's weird, because Anna can be really, really mean. I mostly try to stay away from her.

Cast of

CARLY

CARLY is Anna's best friend. She always tries to act exactly like Anna does. She even wears the exact same clothes. She's never really been mean to me, but she's never been nice to me either!

NICK

NICK is my annoying seven-year-old neighbor. I get stuck babysitting him a lot. He likes to make me miserable. (Okay, he's not that bad ALL of the time . . . just most of the time.)

BRAD

BRAD TURINO is a sports star at our school. He's super nice, too. Plus, he's gorgeous. My deepest, darkest secret is that I have a crush on him. Only Becca and Monica know, and they'd never tell anyone.

Characters

SYLVIA's nice, but we're not that close. She thinks Anna and Carly are so cool. She doesn't realize that they're mean.

SYLVIA

MS. STARK

MS. STARK teaches history, and she's also my homeroom teacher. She doesn't let us get away with much.

CHAPTER 1

ANNA'S BAD IDEA

On Monday morning, homeroom was **noisier** than usual. Everyone had something to say about the seventh-grade dance.

The dance is a big deal at Pine Tree Middle School. It was our first school dance ever. Students had to organize and run the entire dance. **Everybody was talking about it.**

"It has to be a **formal** dance," Anna said.

"What's that?" Carly asked.

"**Fancy** dresses, **pretty** corsages, and **elegant** decorations." Anna's eyes lit up as she talked. "And a band that plays real dance music, like my cousin had at her wedding."

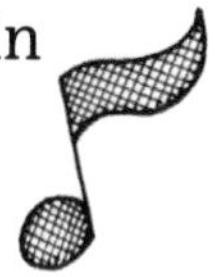

Several kids groaned.

Jenny Pinski made **a face.**

"Are you kidding?" Adam asked. He looked **horrified.** He's been one of my best friends since third grade. I could tell he thought a formal dance was a **terrible** idea.

"No," Anna said. "I've been taking ballroom dance lessons. I want to use what I've learned."

"Why make everyone else suffer?" Monica asked loudly. She's another one of my best friends. She's not afraid to say what she thinks.

Becca, my other best friend, doesn't like to stir up trouble. She whispered to Monica and me, "Anna doesn't care what anyone else wants."

Becca was right about that. Anna is **selfish, spoiled, and extremely popular.** When she doesn't get what she wants, she makes everyone wish they had given in. So Anna almost always gets things her way.

This time had to be different. The dance was too important to the entire seventh grade. **We couldn't let Anna ruin it.**

"A **casual** dance would be nice," I said. "With a D.J. that plays **music we like.**"

"That would be fun," Monica said.

"Ballroom dancing is fun, and it's totally cool," Anna argued. "Don't you ever watch dance contests on TV?"

Monica shook her head. "No," she said. "That sounds totally boring."

The bell rang, and we all took our seats.

"All right, everyone. Who wants to be on the dance committee?" Ms. Stark asked.

Anna raised her hand. "I do. I have some 𝔾ℝ𝔼𝔸𝕋 ideas."

"Me, too!" Carly exclaimed. She does everything Anna does and agrees with everything Anna says.

I never agree with Anna. I raised my hand. "And me!" I said. I nudged Monica, and her hand shot up. Then Becca raised her hand, too.

I crossed my fingers. If the five of us were on the dance committee, the vote would be three against two.

Then Anna couldn't **ruin** the seventh-grade dance.

* * *

I was so nervous at lunch that I could hardly eat. I didn't want Anna to wreck the dance. I had to be on the committee.

Then Ms. Stark came to the cafeteria to announce the dance committee members. When I saw her, **I got so nervous that I gobbled my macaroni and cheese.**

Ms. Stark named Anna and Carly first.

"Fantastic!" Anna yelled. She squealed and hugged Carly.

Then Monica, Becca, and I heard our names called.

"I hope we don't regret this," Monica said.

I knew what she meant. When we voted against a formal dance, **Anna would make us sorry.**

"And Sylvia Sherman," Ms. Stark continued.

"Oh, no!" Anna gasped. "We'll never get anything done with Sylvia on the committee!"

Sylvia is one of those kids who gets **teased a lot.** She really wants to be friends with Anna and the cool kids. I had no doubt that Sylvia would vote with Anna. The committee was split, three to three!

Ms. Stark wasn't finished. "And the seventh member of the dance committee is . . ."

I held my breath. With seven, there couldn't be a tie!

". . . Jenny Pinski."

What?

Jenny was the class bully. **This was not good news.**

TIE BREAKER

We held our first dance committee meeting at Anna's house after school.

Jenny did not want to be there. "I don't know why they're making me be on this committee," Jenny said. "I **hate** this kind of thing."

"Maybe someone else can take your place," I suggested. It seemed like a good idea.

Everyone would be happier, because:

1. Jenny didn't even want to go to the dance. She definitely didn't want to be on the committee.

2. Anna likes being the boss, but nobody can boss Jenny Pinski around.

3. The rest of us didn't want to get on Jenny's bad side.

"I'll make a deal with you, Jenny," Anna said. "If you vote for having a 𝔽𝕆ℝ𝕄𝔸𝕃 dance, you won't have to do anything else for the dance."

Sometimes Anna is really smart. Jenny wouldn't turn that offer down.

"We'll give you the same deal," I said.

"A **D.J.** dance will be a lot more fun," Becca added.

"I think both ideas are **boring,**" Jenny said.

Anna shrugged. "Maybe, but you have  to vote for one or the other. So if you vote for the formal dance, you're off the hook for planning."

Jenny wanted to think about it. We agreed to wait until the next meeting to vote.

Anna wanted a formal dance for three reasons:

1. To show off her ballroom dancing.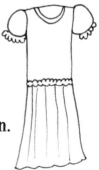

2. To wear a fancy dress.

3. To have her hair done at a beauty salon.

Anna also wanted to get Brad Turino to be her boyfriend.

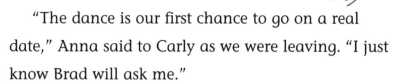

"The dance is our first chance to go on a real date," Anna said to Carly as we were leaving. "I just know Brad will ask me."

Brad is handsome. He's a great athlete, and he's really nice. **I wanted to dance with him more than anything.** That wouldn't happen if he went to the dance with Anna!

After the meeting was over, I felt **sad**. On my way home from Anna's, I stopped at Adam's house.

Adam was BOUNCING a rubber ball off the door of his garage. He **caught** the ball in his baseball glove, and then BOUNCED it again.

"Are you taking a date to the dance?" I asked.

"I'm NOT going to the dance," Adam said.

I blinked. "You're not?"

"Nope." Adam bounced the ball harder. **"None of the guys are going."**

CHAPTER 3

THE BOYS WON'T GO

I couldn't believe what Adam had said. "None of you are going to the dance?" I asked.

Adam nodded. "Nobody wants to go to a **stupid formal dance**. We can't have fun if we have to wear suits."

Did Brad feel that way? **I couldn't dance with him if he stayed home.**

"We haven't decided anything, yet," I said. "Monica, Becca, and I are voting for a D.J. dance."

"You won't win," Adam said. **"Anna always gets her way."**

"Jenny gets the deciding vote," I told him.

"A D.J. won't make any difference to me." Adam sighed. "It doesn't matter. **I don't know how to dance.**"

"You wouldn't have to dance," I argued. "You and your friends could just hang out. There'll be food and soda. Plus, **you don't have to wear a suit** to a D.J. dance."

"That might be okay," Adam said.

I hoped the other boys thought so. I had to find out.

I went to Tommy's house next. He was watching cartoons.

"Are you going to the dance, Tommy?" I asked.

"NOPE," Tommy said.

"Why not?" I asked.

"I can't dance," Tommy admitted. "And **I don't want to look silly.**"

I gasped. "But you try to look silly all the time!"

"I know," Tommy said. "But looking silly on purpose is different than looking silly when you don't mean to."

He had a point.

I found Peter in his backyard. He was counting all the different bugs in one square foot of grass. He didn't know how to dance either.

"I watch those dance shows sometimes with my mom," Peter said. "It looks like fun on TV."

He suddenly grabbed my hand. Then he tried to twirl me. **Our arms got tangled, and we fell down.** I laughed.

"I want to learn," Peter said. "But lessons are too expensive."

"Maybe you could get a DVD that would teach you," I said.

I asked three other boys how they felt about the dance. I realized three things:

1. They didn't want to go to a fancy dance.

2. They might go to a D.J. dance, but only if they didn't have to dance.

3. They didn't want to dance, no matter what.

Two things were crystal clear:

1. If Anna wanted boys to come to the dance, she had to give up her idea of ballroom dancing.

2. If Brad wouldn't go to a formal dance, maybe Anna would change her mind.

So I made a plan:

1. Ask Brad if he liked the idea of a fancy dance. If he didn't, I could tell Anna that, and she would change her mind.

2. Get Jenny to vote for the D.J.

CHAPTER 4

ONE WAY OR THE OTHER

I'm not a perfect person. I have lots of faults.

Sometimes I ask EMBARRASSING questions. Sometimes I do **stupid** things without thinking. One thing bothers me the most: How **nervous** I get when I talk to Brad. Or when I try to talk to Brad. I never get the words out. Not the way I want.

I knew I had to get over it. Brad Turino was just a boy, like Adam or Peter or Tommy. I didn't FREAK OUT when I talked to them.

After dinner, I sat on my bed and stared at  the phone. I had Brad's number written down. I had a good reason to call. **If I didn't do it, I never would.**

I dialed.

Brad answered. "Hello?"

I hung up.

My hands started to sweat, and **my heart thumped.**

I waited a minute to calm down. Then I dialed again.

"Hello?" Brad paused. "Who is this?"

I was RELIEVED. He didn't have Caller ID. I opened my mouth to talk, but no sound came out.

Brad hung up.

I decided it would be easier to talk to him face to face. I'd have to say something if he were standing right in front of me, or **I'd look like a complete fool.**

My chance came first thing the next morning.

I was putting my coat in my locker. I looked up and saw that Brad was walking toward me. He was alone.

All I had to do was smile and say, "Hi, Brad. Can I ask you something?" **Easy, right?**

When Brad got close, I couldn't talk, and I couldn't move. It was like someone had flipped my OFF SWITCH.

Brad smiled at me as he walked by.

I just stared at him. I couldn't smile. My face was frozen.

When Brad turned the corner, I fell back against my locker. I felt a little sick. I had just missed the perfect chance to ask Brad about Anna's plan for the fancy dance.

I never give up. I'd get another chance to talk to Brad before the school day ended. I wouldn't mess it up again.

I had a plan. I wrote a note.

Seventh-grade survey:

Are you going to the dance? Y or N

Even if you have to wear a suit? Y or N

Will you take a date? Y or N

Circle Y or N and return to Claudia Cortez

I kept the paper in my pocket all morning. I didn't want to pass it to Brad in class. If I got caught, the teacher might read it out loud. Then **everyone would think I had a crush on Brad.** I do have a crush on Brad, but only Becca and Monica know about it.

I waited until Brad was in the lunch line.

I didn't have to say much. I just had to give Brad the note.

I took a deep breath and walked toward him. He looked right at me. I kept walking. This time, I didn't have a **goofy look** on my face. I had a FROZEN SMILE.

I was really going to do it. I just had to say, "Here," and give Brad the note. I slowly held out the folded paper.

"Brad!" Anna yelled. She rushed by me, waving her arm. She knocked the note out of my hand. I watched, horrified, as it slid across the cafeteria floor.

For one AWFUL second, I thought Anna would pick it up! If she knew I liked Brad, she'd make it into a big joke. I would be totally **embarrassed**, and Brad would NEVER like me back.

Anna didn't notice my note. She ran right up to Brad. She doesn't have any trouble talking to him.

"Thanks for saving me a place, Brad," Anna said. **She winked at him.**

It's **against the rules** to let friends cut in line. Brad looked surprised, but he let Anna squeeze in. Nobody said anything.

I grabbed my note and walked away. FAST!

* * *

The dance committee was meeting to vote tomorrow. If I wanted answers from Brad, I had to ask the questions today.

Without choking up, running, or babbling.

When the last bell rang, I went to the gym. Brad was in the hall showing Peter a dance step.

"It's not hard. Watch," Brad said. He held a pretend partner and twirled around the floor.

Brad is so cool. I should have guessed that he knew how to dance.

"It looks easy when you do it," Peter said.

Peter and Brad were talking about dancing. I just had to join the conversation. **I paused to calm my nerves.**

"Just loosen up and let yourself go," Brad suggested.

"I'll try. Thanks," Peter said.

Brad went into the gym. Peter walked toward me.

I had let Brad get away again!

"Hi, Claudia," Peter said.

"Is Brad teaching you how to dance?" I asked.

"He was just giving me some pointers," Peter said. **"He takes lessons.** It helps his coordination for sports."

"Does Anna know that?" I asked.

Peter shrugged. "I don't know."

I put the facts together.

1. Brad and Anna both took dance lessons.

2. There was only one dance school in town.

SO: Anna probably knew Brad could dance.

I couldn't tell Anna that Brad couldn't dance and didn't want to go to a formal dance. Anna wouldn't believe me.

That ruined the first part of my plan.

There was only one thing left to do:

1. Convince Jenny to vote for the **D.J.**

CHAPTER 5

FLING FLOP

As soon as I got home, I called Monica and Becca. I asked them to come over. I went to the tree house in my backyard to wait.

Ten minutes later, Monica and Becca climbed into the tree house. They were both out of breath.

"We ran the whole way," Monica said.

"Did something AWFUL happen when you talked to Brad?" Becca asked.

"Not exactly," I said. "I was really **nervous.** I didn't get close enough to ask him anything."

"That's too bad," Becca said. "But at least you didn't get your words all jumbled up."

"That's the only bright side," I said. "Why don't you get **tongue-tied** when you talk to Tommy?"

"Because Tommy doesn't know I like him," Becca said.

"He won't find out from us," Monica promised.

Monica knew I liked Brad and that Becca liked Tommy.

"Who do you want to dance with, Monica?" Becca asked.

Monica shook her head. "I **don't care**. I'll dance with anyone who asks me," she said. "Or I'll dance with friends."

"If Jenny votes for Anna's formal dance, we'll have to dance with friends, because **there won't be any boys** at the dance," I said. "Except for Peter and Brad."

"Why them?" Becca asked.

"Brad can dance, and Peter is learning," I explained.

"So getting the boys to the dance is only **half the problem,**" Becca said.

"What's the other half?" Monica asked.

"The boys won't dance even if they come, because they don't know how," Becca said.

Monica frowned. **"It won't be any fun**
if the boys just stand around."

"We can't force them to dance," I said.

"Right," Monica agreed. "They have to want to."

Becca propped her chin in her hands. "And that's probably IMPOSSIBLE."

That's what I thought too. If the boys didn't go, a formal dance would flop. And the **D.J.** dance would flop if the boys didn't dance.

It seemed like our first seventh-grade dance was going to be our first seventh-grade disaster.

CHAPTER 6

SEARCH FOR A SOLUTION

My dad says that **every problem has a solution.** So there had to be a way to make thirteen-year-old boys want to dance.

After Becca and Monica left, I went inside. Mom was in the kitchen making her YUMMY potato-burger casserole. I asked her, "Mom, did you go to dances when you were my age?"

"YES," Mom said. "Why?"

I sighed. "The boys don't want to go to our dance," I said. "We don't know what to do about it."

"Boys didn't like to dance when I was in junior high, either," Mom said. "But they had to anyway."

"You made them dance?" I perked up. "How?"

"The teachers taught dancing in gym class." Mom shuddered. "It was AWFUL."

"Why?" I asked. I was curious.

"The boys and girls lined up on opposite sides of the gym," Mom said. "Then the gym teacher paired us off into couples."

"That is so not cool." I made a face.

Mom laughed. "I always tried to avoid Richie Conklin, but I always ended up with him."

I had trouble imagining Mom being my age. I couldn't picture her with anyone but my dad.

"Richie had a crush on me," Mom went on. "He'd always count down the line to make sure we matched up."

Just then, NICK ran in the back door.

I frowned. "I didn't know you were watching Nick today, Mom."

Mom sliced a potato. "Just until his mom gets back from the post office."

My mom watches Nick, my seven-year-old neighbor, almost every day. Nick's mom always has something to do, and she usually does it when Nick is home. **I don't think she can stand him either.**

"I want to go to the dance," Nick said.

"You can't," I said. "You're not in seventh grade."

"Don't care." Nick folded his arms and jutted out his chin. "I'm going."

"No, you're not," I said. Nick could throw a dozen tantrums, but he wouldn't get his way about this.

"Am too!" **Nick's eyes flashed.**

"Enough!" Mom said. She stuffed a carrot stick in Nick's mouth.

"**NOT**." I got in the last word and left before Mom asked me to watch Nick. She pays me to watch him, but I had other things to do. Uncle Diego was watching TV in the living room. He comes to our house for dinner a lot.

"What's your mom making, Claudia?" Uncle Diego asked.

"Potato-burger casserole," I said.

"My **favorite.**" Uncle Diego rubbed his stomach.

I sat down on the couch next to him. "Did you go to school dances when you were a kid?" I asked.

"Every single one," Uncle Diego said.

"Really?" **I was surprised.** "Did you like to dance?"

"I don't know." Uncle Diego sighed. "**None of the girls would dance with me**, so I never found out."

"Oh." I felt bad for asking.

"That's why boys don't ask girls to dance," Uncle Diego explained. "It's no fun getting turned down."

"That would be hard," I said.

"Yep." Uncle Diego nodded. "There's only one thing worse. Not getting asked when it's a **lady's choice** song."

"What's lady's choice?" I asked.

"Just what it sounds like," Uncle Diego replied. "That's when **the lady chooses a fellow** to dance with. It's pretty **old-fashioned,** but they still do it at dances sometimes."

I wondered if I could choose **Brad Turino** for a lady's choice dance. I decided to change the subject. "Did Dad go to dances?" I asked.

Uncle Diego laughed. "Your dad was always working or studying. He didn't have time for anything fun like dancing."

I decided I needed to talk to someone who liked dancing. I headed out the front door.

Mr. and Mrs. Gomez live across the street.

"You look **down in the dumps** today, Claudia," Mrs. Gomez said. She and Mr. Gomez were sitting on the porch swing with their little, fluffy dog, Fancy.

"Yeah, I kind of am," I said. I changed the subject. "Did you go to school dances when you were young?"

"We certainly did." Mrs. Gomez smiled at Mr. Gomez. "We loved to be out on the dance floor. Didn't we, dear?"

"We still do!" Mr. Gomez took Mrs. Gomez's hand.

The elderly man and woman clasped hands. They came together, then pushed apart. They held hands on one side and **wiggled** their free hands in the air. They twisted back and forth. Then Mr. Gomez **twirled Mrs. Gomez like Peter tried to twirl me.** But Mr. and Mrs. Gomez didn't get their arms tangled up, and they didn't fall down. **I was amazed.**

"What kind of dance is that?" I asked.

"The JITTERBUG," Mr. Gomez said.

"It was very popular when we were in school," Mrs. Gomez said. She sat back down to catch her breath.

"It's my favorite," Mr. Gomez said. "I might not have married Mrs. Gomez if I hadn't asked her to teach me how."

"He wanted to impress another girl," Mrs. Gomez said.

"I can't even remember her name." Mr. Gomez scratched his head.

"Her name was Dolores," Mrs. Gomez said. She pretended to scowl.

Mr. Gomez ignored his wife and smiled at me. "I didn't know dancing was so much fun until I learned the jitterbug."

Across the street, my mom opened our front door. "Claudia, dinner's ready," she called.

"See you later, Mr. and Mrs. Gomez," I said.

"Come back for dancing lessons any time, Claudia," Mrs. Gomez said. Fancy barked at me.

When I walked into the house, my mom said, "Claudia, please tell Jimmy that it's time for dinner. He's in his room."

My brother, Jimmy, is sixteen. **He doesn't talk to me unless he has to.** And he hates being interrupted when he's in his room playing a computer game.

But Jimmy is a BOY. If there was a way to make boys want to dance, he'd know what it was.

I knocked on his door.

"WHAT?" Jimmy snapped.

I walked in. "Can I ask a question?"

"One question. Hurry up." Jimmy didn't take his eyes off his computer screen. **"I don't want to fall into this river."**

The jungle on the computer screen looked real. Jimmy's character stood on a wooden bridge over a river. It looked like a long way to fall.

"Is that a new game?" I asked.

"It's called **Jungle Safari**." Jimmy smiled. "It just came out, and it's **IMPOSSIBLE** to get. Everybody wants it."

"Did Dad order it for you?" I asked. Our father owns a computer store. He can buy the games at a discount.

"Yes. That's two questions," Jimmy said. "Bye."

I asked a third question before he chased me out. "Did you go to any dances in seventh grade?"

"I didn't want to, but I went." Jimmy moved his character off the bridge and paused the game.

"The committee picked a lame theme. It
was **1970s Dance Fever,**" said Jimmy.

"Why did you decide to go?" I asked.

"That's question number four!" Jimmy frowned.

"Please!" I begged.

Jimmy rolled his eyes and sighed. "Then will you
get lost and leave me alone?"

I crossed my heart. "Promise."

"They offered a **fifty-dollar prize** for
the best disco solo," Jimmy said. "So I
learned to dance and went."

That was all I needed to know.

"Okay. Oh, I almost forgot," I said. "Dinner's
ready."

Jimmy sighed.

CHAPTER 7

Swing Vote

The next day, I walked to Anna's house with Becca and Monica.

"Did you talk to Sylvia, Becca?" I asked.

Becca nodded. "She's not going to vote for a D.J. unless Anna does. Period."

"We know **Carly won't vote against Anna,**" Monica said. "If Jenny votes for a formal dance, that's it. Four against three. Anna wins."

"Jenny told me she was voting for a D.J.," Becca said.

I BLINKED. "Jenny told me she was voting with Anna," I said.

"She told me she hasn't decided yet," Monica said.

"Then we still have a chance," I said.

I just had to convince Jenny to vote for my new idea.

But that was going to be harder than I thought.

When we got to Anna's house, she told us that she wanted us to vote right away.

"But there are things we have to talk about," I said.

"The **boys won't go** to a formal dance," Monica explained quickly.

"**And they won't dance**," Becca said. "Even with a D.J."

I jumped back in. "But we can fix that."

"I really don't want to discuss it," Anna said. "We're having a formal dance."

→ She listed her reasons:

1. She had already bought her dress.

2. She wanted to tango, jitterbug, and waltz.

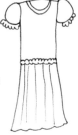

3. She wanted to go with a date, and that date was Brad.

"Sylvia and I are voting with Anna," Carly said.

"I don't care if the boys come and dance or not," Jenny said. "Anna asked for my vote first."

"So there." Anna smiled.

"But I think we can make the boys want to dance!" I exclaimed.

"How?" Carly asked.

"Adam will do **just about anything** to get a new computer game called *Jungle Safari*," I explained.

"So would I," Jenny said. "I can't find it anywhere."

"My dad's store just got more copies," I said. "He'll donate two of them to our dance."

"How can I get one?" Jenny asked.

"We'll have a drawing," I said.

"How will that make boys want to dance?" Sylvia said.

"Couples will have to do **challenges** to be in the drawing," I said. "Like in the game, but our challenges will have dancing. The winners will EACH get a game."

Sylvia and Carly looked at each other. Anna didn't give up.

"Don't you want to **wear pretty dresses?**" Anna asked. **"Or get your hair done at a salon?"**

"No and no," Jenny said.

"I do," Carly said.

"We still can," I said. "We're the dance committee. We'll just say that everyone can wear what they want."

"Then the boys will come, because they won't have to wear suits," Monica added.

Anna wasn't ready to give up. "I want to decorate the gym like a garden, with lots of ELEGANT tables. I have it all planned out."

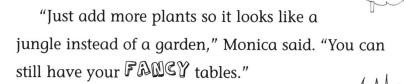

"Just add more plants so it looks like a jungle instead of a garden," Monica said. "You can still have your FANCY tables."

"Yeah." Becca nodded with **excitement.** "We'll call the dance **Safari Swing.**"

Anna rolled her eyes. I knew what she was going to say next, so I beat her to the punch. "We can even ask the **D.J.** to play top-forty songs and ballroom dance music," I said.

Anna didn't look convinced.

"I vote for **Safari Swing,**" Jenny said.

That settled it!

A FEW LITTLE GLITCHES

Safari Swing was the ONLY THING anyone talked about at school the next day. Even Anna was excited. Everyone thought the adventure theme was her idea. I didn't care if she got credit. **Life was much easier when Anna was happy.**

The dance committee had split up into teams to finish the details for the dance. Monica and I were in charge of making up the challenges. "**Are you sure you don't mind** doing refreshments with Sylvia, Becca?" I asked.

"It's better than decorating with Carly and Anna," Becca mumbled.

All our problems with the dance seemed to be solved. The last thing I expected was TROUBLE from Jenny.

The Jenny Jinx: Something always makes Jenny mad. And when Jenny's mad, you better watch out.

Jenny came up to Monica and me at our lockers before class. "I want to help with the challenges," she said.

I was shocked. "Why? We still have a deal," I said. "You voted for the D.J. so you don't have to do anything."

"That's what you wanted, Jenny," Monica added.

"That was before the dance turned into an adventure game with a PRIZE," Jenny said. "I'm going to the dance, and I want to work on the challenges."

I didn't want to argue, because Jenny had a mad look in her eye. She really wanted to help! Why?

It wasn't hard to figure out.

I wanted the challenges to be **easy and fun** so everyone could enter the drawing.

Jenny wanted to make the challenges 𝒽𝒜𝑅𝒟 to keep people out. Then she'd have a better chance of winning the drawing.

That wouldn't be fair.

"We'd love to have your help, Jenny," I said. "But if you help make the challenges, Ms. Stark won't let you compete. It's in the rules." **I tried to look disappointed.**

"Oh." Jenny shrugged. "I'd rather compete."

Monica and I both sighed with 𝑅𝐸𝐿𝐼𝐸𝐹.

* * *

All the girls were 𝒯𝒽𝑅𝐼𝐿𝐿𝐸𝒟 about the new idea for the dance. The boys weren't nearly as excited.

I asked Adam about it at lunch. "Don't the boys want to win the game?"

"Yeah," Adam said. "Even the guys that already have **Jungle Safari** want to try the challenges."

"Then what's the problem?" **I was puzzled.**

"That is the problem!" Adam threw up his 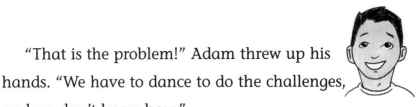 hands. "We have to dance to do the challenges, and we don't know how."

"The video store is out of DVDs that teach you how to dance," Peter said. "I got the last one."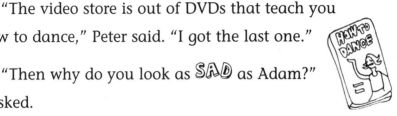

"Then why do you look as SAD as Adam?" I asked.

"I'm not that great at challenges," Peter said.

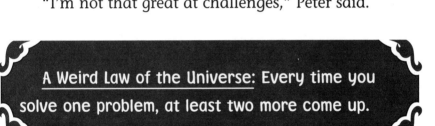

A Weird Law of the Universe: Every time you solve one problem, at least two more come up.

I had forgotten that **not wanting** to dance and not knowing how to dance were two different things. But I had a SOLUTION.

I went to see Coach Johnson and Ms. Campbell. They were the gym teachers.

"Can you teach **all the seventh graders how to dance?**" I asked. "My mom learned to dance in her gym class."

Coach rubbed his chin. "Let us talk about that."

"Okay," I said, "but don't tell anyone it was my idea."

The teachers **promised that they wouldn't.**

I couldn't work on the other problem until I got home. I needed Jimmy's help again.

"What do you want now?" Jimmy asked after I knocked on his door that afternoon.

I explained that the boys expected the dance challenges to be like *Jungle Safari.*

Jimmy didn't yell or complain or chase me away. He pulled another chair up to his computer.

"The first level was a SNAP," Jimmy said. "But there were some cool challenges."

Jimmy is almost as smart as Peter. He's never played a game he couldn't figure out.

I didn't care if Jimmy wanted to show off. He showed me all the challenges in level one. They were a little weird, but I was sure I'd think of something.

Then Jimmy's character had to cross a river of reptiles.

I would **NEVER** be able to convince Anna to **decorate with snakes.**

TOO MANY LEFT FEET

Our gym is split into two halves by a huge folding wall. During gym class, the boys play on one side and the girls on the other. The gym was wide open when we got to class the next day.

"What's going on, Ms. Campbell?" Anna asked.

"We're having class with the boys," Ms. Campbell replied. "So you can all **learn to dance.**"

Almost everyone groaned.

Coach Johnson and Ms. Campbell made the boys and girls line up on opposite sides of the gym. **Anna quickly figured out that the lines would pair off.** She counted down so she was across from Brad.

Monica counted down, too. She moved Becca so that Becca would be with Tommy.

It didn't work.

The coaches started at the other end of the lines.

Peter ended up with Jenny. I danced with Tommy. Monica got Brad. **Anna was furious.**

Coach Johnson and Ms. Campbell showed us the waltz. They looked as **awkward** as I felt. It was hilarious, but nobody laughed.

We all danced liked robots with low batteries.

It wasn't a total loss, though. Since I was dancing with Tommy, **I had a chance to do a good deed for one of my best friends.**

"Becca would be a GREAT PARTNER for the challenges, Tommy," I said.

"Why?" Tommy asked. He looked interested.

"She's a good dancer," I said. "Plus, she really wants to win the game."

That was only **half a lie.** Becca didn't play computer games, but Tommy did. Becca liked Tommy, so she wanted to help him win.

"You could even practice before you try the challenges," I suggested. "Then you might get extra tickets for the drawing."

"How?" Tommy asked.

That was part of my **master plan** to make the boys dance.

When a couple completed a challenge, an adult would write both names on a ticket for the drawing. If the couple danced really well, the adult could give them two tickets. **That meant they had even better chances of winning.**

"Thanks for the 𝕋𝕀ℙ," Tommy said. "I'll remember that."

"It's time to tango!" Coach Johnson yelled. "That's tango! Not tangled. You all dance like you've got two left feet."

"We do!" Tommy called out. **"My left foot plus Claudia's left foot equals two left feet!"**

"That was a good one, Tommy!" Adam laughed.

Coach Johnson and Ms. Campbell demonstrated the basic tango.

"I can do that," Tommy said. **"I saw it on Peter's DVD."**

I put one hand on Tommy's shoulder. He put one hand on my waist. Our other hands were together. We pushed our clasped hands out so that our arms stuck straight to the right.

Tommy turned his head and stared at our hands. **Then he yelled, "Charge!"**

Everyone laughed as Tommy and I barreled across the gym.

It was embarrassing, but at least **it was FUNNY**.

MORE DECISIONS

At the next dance committee meeting, Anna was in a bad mood.

"We've got lots of volunteers to help decorate," Carly said. "And my mom donated paper tablecloths."

Sylvia slowly raised her hand.

"What?" Anna asked impatiently.

Sylvia began, "I called Wilson's . . ."

Anna finished Sylvia's sentence. "Wilson's Nursery is loaning us bunches of potted plants. Anything else?"

"I only found four toy stores that have plastic snakes," Monica said. "And they don't have very many."

"Good! I HATE the idea of using **snakes!**" Anna said angrily.

"The game has a **river of reptiles,**" I explained. "So the dance needs one, too."

"The boys will love it," Monica said.

"Besides," Becca added, "we're putting the challenges in the hall. There won't be any snakes in the gym."

"WHATEVER." Anna sighed.

"We need **hundreds** of snakes," Jenny said. "Or we'll have a **puddle** of reptiles, not a RIVER. That's not good enough."

Sylvia raised her hand again. "I have an idea. **Everyone could bring a snake to the dance,**" she said.

"Like a ticket?" Monica asked.

"That's a great idea, Sylvia!" I exclaimed.

"So each person has to bring a snake to get in. And if they don't have a snake, they can bring plastic spiders or frogs or even alligators," Becca said.

"That still won't be enough," Jenny said.

Nobody argued with Jenny. We all agreed to find creepy crawly toys.

Then Becca made another suggestion. "We should have three lady's choice dances."

"Yeah!" Carly shouted.

Everyone agreed, even Jenny. We looked at her in surprise.

"I want to **test different partners for the challenges,**" Jenny explained.

Anna just wanted the meeting to be over. "Is that all?" she asked.

"I guess so," Becca said. "Sylvia and I have everything we need for the refreshment table."

"Then this meeting is over," Anna said.

I couldn't wait to leave. Anna is never easy to be around. **It's worse when she's upset.**

"Did Brad ask you to the dance, Anna?" Carly asked.

"Not yet," Anna snapped. "But he will."

"No, he won't," Monica said.

"How would you know?" Anna sneered.

"I danced with Brad in gym class, remember?" Monica smiled. She loves getting the best of Anna. "He told me **the sports guys aren't taking dates.**"

Anna was so **MAD** she couldn't talk.

I was **speechless** with **DELIGHT**.

Brad wasn't taking a date! So I could ask him to dance!

If I could get the words out.

CHAPTER 11

FINAL DETAILS

I'm not a fancy and elegant person like Anna. But I LOVED my new dress.

It was the **prettiest** thing I'd ever worn. The dress was bubble-gum pink. It had a SWINGY, soft skirt that hung above my knees. Mom even let me splurge on shiny, hot-pink shoes that showed off my toes.

I would look **grown-up and elegant,** but I could still move to dance, and I wouldn't wobble when I walked.

I put my dress on a hanger and hung it up in the closet. I didn't want cat hair all over it.

Whenever I get something new, my cat, Ping-Ping, takes a nap on it.

Then I went to see Mrs. Gomez. Over the past week, she had taught me to **jitterbug, waltz,** and **tango.** I was using all three dances in the challenges.

"I want pictures of your challenges," Mrs. Gomez said.

"I'll have video," I said. Several teachers were bringing cameras.

"Let's run through this one more time." Mrs. Gomez put a record on her old-fashioned record player.

"The jitterbug!" I exclaimed. "My **favorite.**"

Mrs. Gomez and I wiggled and jiggled, twisted and twirled. Fancy barked at my heels.

"You'll win that contest for sure," Mrs. Gomez said when the song ended.

"I designed the challenges, so I can't do them," I said.

"Then why did you work so hard?" Mrs. Gomez asked.

"I have my reasons," I said. I BLUSHED. Mrs. Gomez didn't know about Brad.

* * *

By dinnertime that night, I was almost done with everything I had to do.

But the third challenge needed a tribal warrior, and I still didn't have one. **No one at Pine Tree Middle School wanted the job.**

I had some good luck with the creepy reptiles and bugs, though. Nick's mom, Mrs. Wright, had said I could look through Nick's toy box. **Unfortunately,** she hadn't told Nick.

"You're not going to STEAL my toys, Claudia!" Nick yelled, standing between his toy box and me. He was wearing the helmet from his Halloween knight costume and waving a foam sword.

"I just want to BORROW them," I said.

"Back!" Nick lunged at me.

"Your mother said I could take them!" I said, glaring at him.

"Don't care." **Nick glared back.**

"Too bad." I took a step toward him.

"Too bad for you!" Nick whacked me with the foam sword.

It didn't hurt, but **I backed off.** I've known Nick for a long time. There's only one way to get him to do what I want.

BRIBE HIM.

I looked Nick in the eye and asked, "Do you still want to go to the seventh-grade dance?"

CHAPTER 12

DANCE CHALLENGE

Everyone on the dance committee was in the gym when I arrived. Monica and I had finished setting up the challenges at six o'clock. We barely had time to race home and change.

"I love your dress!" Becca said.

I loved how the gym looked. It was full of potted plants. Fake vines hung on wooden arches. The round tables each had a white tablecloth and a basket of flowers. Anna and Carly had even put African masks and drums around the room.

"Wow!" I exclaimed. "The decorations are FANTASTIC."

"Everything I do is fantastic," Anna said.

I ignored her. "It's **exactly** like the scenes in **Jungle Safari**," I said.

The **D.J.** was setting up on the stage. Coach Johnson sat in a corner with a TV and DVD player. He had a DVD called **"Learn to Dance the Fun and Easy Way!"** Kids could watch the DVD before they tried the challenges.

I walked over to check out the refreshment table. Sylvia was standing behind the long table, which was covered with different kinds of treats and drinks.

"Have a **zebra ear**," Sylvia said. She held out a plate of cookies. They had stripes of vanilla and chocolate icing.

All the snacks had jungle names. The fruit punch was **bug juice**. Cupcakes with white icing and chocolate sprinkles were called **ant delights**. A **lava melt** was nachos with cheese dip.

"The names were Sylvia's idea," Becca said.

"Claudia!" Anna yelled. "They're coming!" I looked over, and saw about a dozen kids walking in.

Half the boys came in **safari costumes**. Most of the girls wore fancy dresses. Jenny was dressed like a treasure hunter with a floppy hat and scuffed boots.

Monica and I called the first challenge **Dancing With Snakes**.

The floor was covered with a blue tarp. We had used wooden landscape borders and potted plants to make a winding riverbed. We piled snakes along the sides and put a WATERFALL at the exit.

Mr. Chen, the biology teacher, was in charge of the first challenge. He pointed to the dance diagram we'd made on the riverbed with footprint stickers. **"Just follow the footprints,"** he said.

Waltz music played on little speakers. It was just loud enough for the first couple on the challenge to hear.

The boy tried to follow the pattern, but he stumbled. When they finished, Mr. Chen wrote their names on a ticket and put it in a jar.

The next challenge was called THE SWARM.

The floor was bare except for a few potted plants. A film of swarming soldier ants showed on a large video screen. Jitterbug music played on another set of speakers.

"**Millions of ants** sweep over the ground," Mr. Palmer, our principal, said in a deep voice, reading a script I had written. "They eat everything in their path."

"What are we supposed to do?" A boy asked.

"Get from this side of the challenge to the other side without being **eaten by a million ants,**" Mr. Palmer said.

The girl watched the ants on the TV screen and squirmed. "How?" she asked.

"Dance very fast," the teacher said.

Ms. Campbell, the gym teacher, was the adult in charge of the third challenge, **Tango for Rubies.** In the *Jungle Safari* game, the characters have to steal a ruby from an ancient city. At Safari Swing, couples had to carry a red relay flag and tango. But there was a catch.

Nick guarded the red flags with his foam sword.

"How do I look, Claudia?" Nick held out his arms.

"Very cool, Nick," I said. Nick wanted to wear his Halloween knight costume. He drives a hard bargain for a kid.

Ms. Campbell told the first couple what to do and turned on the music.

"That's your cue, Nick," I said. I stepped back.

Nick lowered the plastic visor on his helmet. He stood between the couple and a container of red flags.

The teenage boy picked up another foam sword. He and Nick had a sword fight.

WHACK! WHACK! WHACK!

The girl ran around them and grabbed a flag. Then the boy dropped his sword.

The couple held the red flag in their outstretched hands. They did the **tango** across the room and dropped the flag in a big box. Then Ms. Campbell wrote out their drawing ticket.

As more and more kids danced, I moved from one challenge to another helping out. I replaced pens that ran out of ink and kept the snakes pushed to the side of the riverbed. Then I took a break to watch Peter and Jenny dance through **The Swarm.**

They were a **perfect team**. Peter was a great dancer, and Jenny was determined to win. They did a **crazy jitterbug** across the room.

The teacher gave them two tickets for the drawing. Jenny gave Peter a **high five.**

I was **so busy** working on the challenges that I almost forgot a dance was going on in the other room.

Then Monica rushed out. "Come on!" she said, grabbing my arm. "The D.J. just said **the next dance will be lady's choice!**"

CHAPTER 13

BRAD JITTERS

Monica and I rushed into the gym.

Tommy and Becca were standing by the refreshment table. When the D.J. said that the next dance was lady's choice, **Becca didn't move!** Good thing Tommy didn't wait to be asked.

"Come on," he said to Becca. "We need to **practice.**" He yanked Becca onto the dance floor.

"Okay, Claudia," Monica said. "Your turn."

I followed Monica to the corner where Brad was standing with his friend Jake. When I didn't say anything, Monica did.

"Come on, Jake," Monica said. "You're dancing with me."

"Oh, no!" Jake joked. He laughed as they walked away.

Brad smiled at me. I opened my mouth, but my voice wouldn't come out. I coughed to clear my throat.

Then I heard Anna's voice. "There you are!" she yelled. She ran over, grabbed Brad's hand, and pulled him onto the dance floor.

Anna didn't ask. She didn't give Brad a chance to say no. She knew what she wanted, and she took it. Right out from under my nose.

I didn't want to watch Anna and Brad dance, so I went back to the challenges. Everyone was having a great time, except Nick.

"What's the matter?" I asked.

"I can't win a fight!" Nick frowned. "All these guys are bigger than me. And **Mom said I couldn't kick them.**"

"Good!" Adam exclaimed. He and Sylvia were the next couple in line.

"I bet I can beat you," Nick said to Adam. He raised his sword.

Adam whispered something to Sylvia. Then he picked up the other foam sword. **He lunged at Nick, and the battle was on.**

But Adam and Sylvia weren't playing to win. Sylvia moved really slowly on purpose. She didn't grab a flag. **Adam let Nick whack the sword out of his hand.**

"Yippee!" Nick whooped. "**I won! I won!**"

Adam sighed. "Well, now we can't tango for the drawing."

"That's okay. We have other tickets," Sylvia said.

Adam and Sylvia had given up their third chance in the drawing to make Nick happy. **I thought that was really nice.**

Of course, Nick didn't stay happy for long. After he lost the next battle, he threw his cup of bug juice at me. Some of it landed on my dress.

When the D.J. called the second lady's choice, I was in the restroom **washing bug juice off my dress.** The dance was over by the time I got back to the gym.

Anna had danced with Brad. Again.

"It's no big deal," Monica said. "He's walking away."

I made myself look at them. Brad walked away from Anna the instant the **music changed.**

"He left right away when the first lady's choice was over, too," Monica said. "I just know he'll say yes if you ask."

I had one more chance to find out.

CHAPTER 14

SAVE THE LAST DANCE

When everyone had finished the challenges, I took Nick to the refreshment table. "Have some bug juice," I said. "Since you spilled your last cup on me."

"I don't want juice made from bug guts." **Nick gagged.**

"It's fruit punch," Sylvia explained.

I held out a cupcake. "And **these aren't really ants.**"

Nick scowled, but he took the drink and cupcake.

The music stopped, and the D.J. held up his hands. "This is the big moment, folks!"

The teachers walked over with the jars from the challenges. They dumped all the tickets into a big box. **The D.J. closed his eyes.** Then he put his hand in the box.

"I hope I win," Nick said.

"You don't have any tickets in the drawing," I said.

"But I want a game!" Nick's eyes flashed. **He was going to throw a tantrum.** I had to stop him before he ruined the drawing.

I blurted out the first bribe that popped into my head. "I'll take you to the park every day next week if you don't kick and scream."

"Okay," Nick said. He shrugged. **That was too easy.**

"And the winners are . . ." The D.J. unfolded the paper. **"Jenny Pinski and Peter Wiggins!"**

Jenny squealed. Peter's mouth fell open. Then they both ran on stage.

The D.J. gave them each a *Jungle Safari* game. 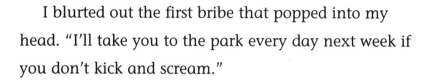 **Everyone cheered and applauded.**

"I'm sorry we didn't win, Tommy," Becca said.

"Yeah, but I had fun trying." Tommy grinned.

"Me, too." Becca giggled.

Then the D.J. announced the **last lady's choice dance.** I didn't see any of my friends anywhere.

Brad was by the stage talking to Peter. I had to ask now or lose my last chance to dance with him.

I saw Anna rushing across the gym toward Brad.

I was too late.

Monica suddenly appeared by Brad's side. She whispered in his ear. Brad nodded and walked behind her toward the refreshment table.

Anna ran after him. Monica walked over to me when Anna stopped Brad.

MY HEART SANK.

But then Brad walked away from Anna. She looked shocked. So was I!

"Why didn't Anna ask Brad to dance?" I asked Monica.

"She probably did," Monica said. "But I asked him to dance first. **With you.**"

"Huh?" I blinked.

"I'm a lady, and that's my choice." Monica grinned.

I was so surprised! I didn't say anything when Brad walked up. I just let him lead me onto the dance floor.

This time, the lady's choice was a FAST SONG. That was okay. We danced so fast we couldn't talk. So I didn't stutter or choke up! I didn't stumble, either. Thanks to Mrs. Gomez's lessons, **my feet worked exactly the way they were supposed to.**

The song ended way too soon.

"This is the last dance," the D.J. said. He played a slow song. All the couples around us started dancing. I expected Brad to walk away from me like he walked away from Anna.

"Can I have this dance, too, Claudia?" Brad asked.

I was so stunned that I gasped. I couldn't talk. I just nodded. **My insides felt like mush when Brad took my hand.**

After the song, everyone was sad because the dance was almost over.

I couldn't stop smiling!

CHAPTER 15

P.S.

Everyone — teachers, parents, and students — agreed that Safari Swing was the *BEST* seventh-grade dance ever. Anna took all the credit, but I didn't mind. **I had danced with Brad Turino. Twice!** And he asked me!

I still can't talk to Brad. He smiles when I see him in the hall, but that doesn't mean anything. **He's a nice guy, and he smiles at everyone.**

Jenny was so happy that she won the ***Jungle Safari*** game. She told Peter she'd never ever stomp him —unless he makes her really, really mad.

I saved my allowance and babysitting money for a month to buy ***Jungle Safari*** for Adam. I wanted to thank him for **being so nice to Nick.** My dad gave me a discount.

My dad gave Nick's mom a discount on the **_Jungle Safari_** game too. She bought it for Nick, since he was a fantastic warrior, and he didn't mess up once. And that proves something else my dad always says: **Nothing is impossible.**

The End

About the Author

Diana G. Gallagher lives in Florida with her husband and five dogs, four cats, and a cranky parrot. Her hobbies are gardening, garage sales, and grandchildren. She has been an English equitation instructor, a professional folk musician, and an artist. However, she had aspirations to be a professional writer at the age of twelve. She has written dozens of books for kids and young adults.

About the Illustrator

Brann Garvey grew up in the great state of Iowa, where he studied art and visual communications. He graduated from the Minneapolis College of Art and Design with a degree in illustration. Brann is usually found with one or more of the following: a pencil in his hand, a comic book, a remote for watching DVDs, or his pet kitty, Iggy. When the weather is nice, Brann likes to play disc golf, and he proudly points out that Iowa is one of the world's centers for the sport. Iggy does not play.

Glossary

awkward (AWK-wurd)—difficult or embarrassing

casual (KAZH-oo-uhl)—not formal, relaxed

challenge (CHAL-uhnj)—something that is difficult

committee (kuh-MIT-ee)—a group of people chosen to make decisions for a larger group

convince (kuhn-VINSS)—make someone believe or agree to something

corsage (kor-SAHJ)—a small bouquet of flowers

elegant (EL-uh-guhnt)—graceful and stylish, fancy

formal (FOR-muhl)—proper, fancy, not casual

jitterbug (JIH-tur-bug)—a popular dance from the 1940s

old-fashioned (ohld-FASH-uhnd)—no longer popular, from another time

regret (ri-GRET)—to be sorry or sad about something

safari (suh-FAH-ree)—a trip to see large, exotic animals

swing (SWING)—a form of dance to lively jazz music

tango (TAYNG-go)—a kind of ballroom dance

waltz (WALTS)—a smooth, gliding ballroom dance

Discussion Questions

1. Has your school had any dances? How did you feel about them? Were they fun, or not? If your school hasn't had a dance, do you like the idea of having one?

2. Anna usually gets her own way, but she doesn't in this book. How did Claudia and her friends convince Anna to compromise? What are some other things they could have done?

3. In this book, at first, the boys don't want to go to the dance. What are their reasons for not going? How would you feel about going to the dance?

Writing Prompts

1. The theme for the dance in this book is Safari Swing. Create your own theme for a dance. What would you call it? How would you decorate? What kind of music would you choose? Write about it.

2. In this book, Claudia gets dance lessons from her neighbor, Mrs. Gomez. Write about a time that an older person helped you learn something.

3. Claudia gets nervous around Brad. She has a hard time talking to him, even though she's friends with other boys. Is there anyone you feel nervous around? Write about a time when you had to talk to that person. How did you feel? What happened?

MORE FUN
with Claudia!

Claudia Cristina Cortez

Just like every other thirteen-year-old girl, Claudia Cristina Cortez has a complicated life. Whether she's studying for the big Quiz Show, babysitting her neighbor, Nick, avoiding mean Jenny Pinski, planning the seventh-grade dance, or trying desperately to pass the swimming test at camp, Claudia goes through her complicated life with confidence, cleverness, and a serious dash of cool.

Internet Sites

Do you want to know more about subjects related to this book? Or are you interested in learning about other topics? Then check out FactHound, a fun, easy way to find Internet sites.

Our investigative staff has already sniffed out great sites for you!

Here's how to use FactHound:

1. Visit *www.facthound.com*

2. Select your grade level.

3. To learn more about subjects related to this book, type in the book's ISBN number: **1598898418**.

4. Click the **Fetch It** button.

FactHound will fetch the best Internet sites for you!

DATE DUE			

FIC
GAL

Gallagher, Diana G.

Dance trap